MY FANTASTIC FIELDTRIP
• JUNIOR DISCOVERS SAVING •

BY DAVE RAMSEY
ILLUSTRATED BY MARSHALL RAMSEY

Dedication

To my Daniel – I hope you always keep your passion for life, love of drawing and sense of humor. It will take you far.
To my baby David – I hope you always have your quick smile, happy personality and infectious laugh.
You'll achieve greatness if you do.

I am a changed man because of both of you. And I will always see your mother's beauty in your deep blue eyes.
Love, Dad (Marshall)

www.daveramsey.com

 The children's group of Lampo Press

My Fantastic Fieldtrip: Junior Discovers Saving
Copyright © 2003 by Lampo Group, Inc.

Requests for information should be addressed to:
Lampo Press: 1749 Mallory Lane Suite #100, Brentwood, Tennessee 37027

ISBN 0-9726323-3-6

First Edition

Written by: Dave Ramsey
Editors: Charlene Kever, Debbie LoCurto, LeeAnne Blair, Amber Frey and Darrin Dickey
Cover Design and Art Direction: Marshall Ramsey

Printed by Vaughan Printing
Printed in the United States of America

For more information on Dave Ramsey, go to: www.daveramsey.com or call (888) 227-3223
For more information on Marshall Ramsey, go to: www.clarionledger.com/ramsey

Today was not a typical day at school. TODAY was the day of the FANTASTIC FIELDTRIP to the Dollar Bill show. Junior had waited so long. His favorite TV show was Dollar Bill's Adventures! And now Junior was going to meet Dollar Bill!

Junior heard the school bell and then the loud speaker hummed to life . . . "Good morning, Children, this is Principal Woodburn. As you know today is the day of the FANTASTIC FIELDTRIP to Dollar Bill's Adventures! We will be loading the buses in 15 minutes. I am asking that you form a straight line and that each of you talk with your 'inside' voices during the bus loading procedure. I look forward to going on this fieldtrip with you today and will be dismissing each class to load the bus shortly."

Junior raised his hand and asked his teacher, Ms. Harper, if he might lead the line to the bus. "Yes, Junior, you may lead our class," answered Ms. Harper.

Junior walked to the front of the room to start the line. Billy ran to stand right behind Junior and soon the entire class was lined up to load on the bus.

Principal Woodburn came to the door and asked, "Ms. Harper, is your class ready to go?"

"Yes, sir!" replied Junior, answering for Ms. Harper.

"Well, Junior you seem very excited to go to Dollar Bill's Adventure show."

"Yes, sir, Principal Woodburn!" exclaimed Junior, "Dollar Bill's Adventures is my favorite TV show!"

"Well, lead the way to the bus," said Principal Woodburn.

Junior led his class down the hall and out the door to the school bus.

Soon the bus took off, and they were on their way to Dollar Bill's Adventures. "How do you know so much about the Dollar Bill show?" asked Erica, one of Junior's friends. Before Junior could answer, Billy leaned across the aisle and said in a TV star voice, "It's about life, love and the pursuit of PILES OF CASH." All the children began laughing.

"Well, Erica," replied Junior, "Dollar Bill does talk about money, but he teaches you how to take care of your money so your money will take care of you!"

Principal Woodburn joined in, "Yes, children, just like Ms. Harper teaches you to read, to count and do your math, Dollar Bill teaches us about how to use our money in the best way as we get older."

"There's Dollar Bill's studio!" cried Esther. Right up the road was a BIG building with a sign that read 'Dollar Bill's Adventures.'

"Hurray! WooHoo!" yelled the children.

The bus came to a stop in the parking lot. Principal Woodburn and Ms. Harper had all the children form a straight line. Junior was still leading the group with Billy next in line. The children walked into the building and went into a big room that had a lot of chairs and a platform up front.

They had just been seated when suddenly a voice boomed from the speakers saying, "Please welcome to the stage America's most trusted financial hero, Dollar Bill!" All the children jumped to their feet and applauded and cheered. Junior jumped the highest and yelled the loudest!

Dollar Bill burst onto the platform and said, "Hello, boys and girls. Welcome to Dollar Bill's Adventures! I'm glad you are here today. We have a lot to learn about money!"

"How many of you earn money by doing chores around the house or helping your neighbors? Or maybe you get money for your birthday and you save it in a big piggy bank in your room?" asked Dollar Bill. Almost all of the children raised their hands.

"Good," said Dollar Bill, "we are going to learn how to take care of your money so your money can take care of you!"

"Let's say I can earn five dollars for making my bed and doing my chores ALL week. I work very hard and at the end of the week I have five one dollar bills," said Dollar Bill. He pulled some money out of his pocket and counted, "One, two, three, four, five. What is the very first thing I need to do with my money?" asked Dollar Bill.

"We need to give some money to help others!" Cristina yelled.

"Exactly," said Dollar Bill, and he placed one dollar in an envelope marked G-I-V-E. "We need to GIVE money to help others!"

"What is something else you can do with your money?" asked Dollar Bill.

Erica yelled out, "Buy toys!"

"Yes," replied Dollar Bill, "you can buy toys." And he put one dollar in an envelope marked S-P-E-N-D. "When we want to buy something, we need to have money to SPEND."

"But there is another envelope that we need to put money in BEFORE we start spending. Can anyone think of what envelope that might be?" asked Dollar Bill.

Junior jumped to his feet and yelled out, "You need an envelope to SAVE money!"

"You're right, young man," said Dollar Bill, "you must have an envelope marked SAVE!" Dollar Bill's favorite helper Lara Mayes, the AMAZING ONE, climbed onto the platform with a BIG envelope marked S-A-V-E and handed it to Dollar Bill.

"YOU MUST SAVE MONEY!" said Dollar Bill. Then he took three dollars and placed them in the SAVE envelope.

"Let's see if you can help me figure out WHY we need to SAVE money! What would happen if you spent ALL of your money on toys and then your teacher needed you to buy some school supplies?" asked Dollar Bill.

"You would not be able to get the proper school supplies that your teacher requested," replied Principal Woodburn, "because you would not have any money to purchase them."

"That's right," said Dollar Bill. "And if you couldn't get your supplies for school because you had spent ALL your money on toys, that would be sad!" said Dollar Bill. "You need to save money for an EMERGENCY . . . that's when something happens that you are not expecting, but you need to be ready for!"

"My grandmother says, 'You need a rainy day fund,'" said Dollar Bill as he popped open a BIG RED UMBRELLA. "Just like when it rains we need an umbrella, when we have an emergency we need an EMERGENCY FUND," explained Dollar Bill. "We need to put some money in the SAVE envelope for emergencies."

"There is one more reason we need to SAVE money. Can anyone think of it?" asked Dollar Bill.

None of the children knew the answer. They had learned to GIVE some of their money to help others. They knew to take some of their money and SPEND it on things they needed and wanted. "Why do we need to SAVE money?" they wondered.

"I don't know, Dollar Bill," said Tiffany. "Tell us why we need to SAVE money!"

Dollar Bill said, "You need to SAVE money for your future! When you get to be a BIG kid you may want to buy a car or go to college. So, you need to SAVE money for when you get BIG!!"

Again, Lara Mayes, the AMAZING ONE, came to the platform. This time she had a BIG sign. The sign read "BEN" and "ARTHUR." Dollar Bill pointed to "BEN" and said, "Take a look at BEN. He started saving money when he was VERY, VERY young. BEN saved his chore money and did not SPEND it all."

"But ARTHUR did not save when he was very young; he waited until he was a BIG, BIG boy. And look what happened, boys and girls," said Dollar Bill, "BEN saved enough money to buy a car when he got BIG, while ARTHUR was still walking!"

"WOW!" thought Junior, "I want to have a CAR when I get big!"

"So, don't forget . . . YOU MUST SAVE MONEY, and you need to start right NOW," said Dollar Bill.

GIVE
SAVE
SPEND

"Today I have taught you to take care of your money in three envelopes ... GIVE, SAVE and SPEND. Your assignment is to go home tonight and get your envelopes started! START SAVING!"

Dollar Bill waved goodbye and all the children screamed, "Thank you, Dollar Bill!"

"Well, boys and girls, didn't we have a wonderful time at Dollar Bill's Adventures?" asked Ms. Harper.

"YES!" screamed all the children. Then, Principal Woodburn had the children form a straight line and they loaded back onto the school bus.

Later that evening, Junior told his parents about his day. Junior said, "Today we had a FANTASTIC FIELDTRIP to Dollar Bill's Adventures. I learned SO much."

"What did you learn, Junior?" asked Dad.

Junior pulled ALL his money out of his pocket and placed it on the table and asked his mom for three envelopes. Then Junior explained what he learned on his FANTASTIC FIELDTRIP.

On the first envelope he wrote G-I-V-E. "Dollar Bill said we need one envelope for giving!" And Junior placed a couple of dollars in his giving envelope so he might help others.

On the second envelope he wrote S-P-E-N-D. "Dollar Bill told us to put money in this envelope so we'll have money when we go to buy something," said Junior. And then Junior placed a few of his chore dollars in the spending envelope so he would have money to get toys and school supplies.

Finally, Junior took the third envelope and wrote S-A-V-E. "Before we SPEND money, Dollar Bill taught us to add money to this envelope. I need to SAVE money for a 'rainy day,' you know, an EMERGENCY – so I'll be ready when something unexpected happens." So, Junior placed a few dollars in his savings envelope.

Then Junior said, "I need to SAVE money for one more thing."

"What's that?" asked Mom.

"I need to SAVE money for my CAR," announced Junior. "Dollar Bill says I need to save money for the things I want in the future when I get to be a BIG kid! And that I need to start NOW and not be walking like ARTHUR!"

Both of Junior's parents began to laugh. "Yes, Junior," said Dad, "you need to SAVE, and you need to start NOW!"

Junior placed a couple MORE dollars in his SAVE envelope and began to laugh with his mom and dad.

Junior hugged his parents and said, "Good night." He picked up his three envelopes – GIVE, SAVE and SPEND and took them to his room. As he climbed into bed, he thought about all that Dollar Bill had said. Junior decided, "No matter what, I'm going to SAVE money for my future – when I get to be a BIG kid!"

Soon Junior was fast asleep
dreaming about the car he will
buy when he gets BIG!